Usborne
Sticker Dollies
Mermaid in Trouble

Zanna Davidson

Illustrated by Heather Burns
Cover illustration by Antonia Miller

Use the stickers to dress the Dolls on the 'Meet the Dolls' pages

Meet the Magic Dolls

Grace, Lily and Holly are the 'Magic Dolls'.
They care for the magical creatures, from
unicorns to fairies and mermaids, that live
on the Enchanted Isle.

Holly

has a special relationship
with the trees and woodland
creatures in the Spellwood. She
also loves the mermaids that
live by the Sparkling Shore.

Lily

has a passion for
flowers and fairies. She is
brilliant at healing magical
creatures with her herbs
and flower potions.

Grace

is fascinated by all
magical creatures.
She reads books on how to
care for them and spends
as much time as she can
on the Enchanted Isle.

Dolly Town

The Magic Dolls live in Honeysuckle Cottage, in Dolly Town, home to all the Dolls. The Dolls work in teams to help those in trouble and are the very best at what they do, whether that's fashion design, ice skating or puppy training. Each day brings with it an exciting new adventure…

The **Shooting Star** train whisks the Dolls away on their missions.

Madame Coco's Costume Emporium has everything the Dolls might need.

The Dolls love to celebrate at the **Cupcake Café.**

Animal Sanctuary

Rose Theatre

Bluebell Bookshop

Evergreen Sports Arena

Royal Palace

Palm Tree Film Studios

HEARTBEAT

Fashion Design Studio

Heartbeat Dance Academy

Mission Control Centre lets the Dolls know who's in trouble and where to go.

Pop Star Stadium

Sparkles

Silver Sparkles Skating Rink

Strawberry Lane Stables

Honeysuckle Cottage is home to the Magic Dolls.

Chapter One

A Secret Mission

T he Magic Dolls were
gathered in the kitchen of
Honeysuckle Cottage.
Holly was deep in
her book about
mermaids.

"I do hope we get to meet the mermaids again soon," Holly said with a sigh.

"Don't get your hopes up too much," said Lily, gently. "Remember that they're really shy."

"I know," said Holly. "Aren't they amazing though?" And she held up her book for the others to see.

"Wow!" said Grace. "Although I still think unicorns are the most magical creatures of all…"

Mermaids are
shy and secretive.
Their ruler is the
Mer Queen, who lives
in a Seashell Palace in
the Undersea Kingdom.

"Grace, you'll love this then,"
said Holly, turning the page.

UNICORN OF THE SEA

Unicorns of the Sea have long,
pearly horns that gleam, even in dark
waters. They are friendly creatures
that love to be patted and stroked.

"A Unicorn of the Sea!" gasped Grace. "Wouldn't it be amazing to see one?" But before the other Dolls could answer, their watches started flashing.

"It's Mission Control!" cried Lily. "They must have a new mission for us. Come in, Mission Control," she said, tapping the symbol on her watch.

There's a mermaid in TROUBLE.
Her name is Nerissa.
She needs you to come quickly.
She says it's top secret and she'll explain when you get there. Can you help?

Holly was jumping up and down with excitement.

HOORAY!
A mermaid mission!

"I think Holly's saying we'd love to help," laughed Lily. "Please tell Nerissa we'll be there as soon as we can."

"Thank you!" said Mission Control. "Sending through the mission details now."

MISSION LOCATION:

The Enchanted Isle

Fairy Palace

Fairy Ring

Silver Stream

Spellwood

Pixie Meadows

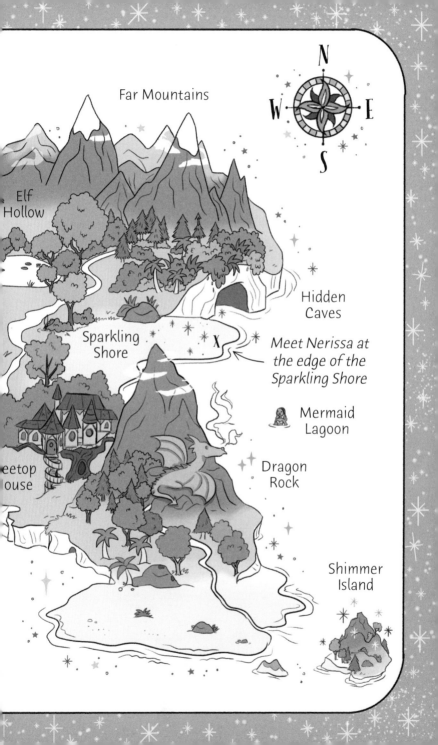

Far Mountains

Elf Hollow

Hidden Caves

Sparkling Shore

X

Meet Nerissa at the edge of the Sparkling Shore

Mermaid Lagoon

Dragon Rock

eetop ouse

Shimmer Island

Mermaid in trouble

Mission details:

Meet at the edge of the
Sparkling Shore.

Mission is TOP SECRET.
Nerissa does not want the
Mer Queen to know about it.

This mission takes place underwater.

You will need to visit the
Undersea Kingdom.

NERISSA THE MERMAID

Sparkling seashell hair clip

Green eyes

Long, wavy dark hair

A top decorated with shining sea flowers

Shimmering pink and blue tail

"Details received," replied Grace, and turned to the others. "But *how* are we going to help?" she wondered aloud. "We can't breathe underwater, or swim as fast as a mermaid…"

"Let's go to Madame Coco's Costume Emporium," suggested Lily. "Madame Coco always has everything we need."

When the Magic Dolls arrived at Madame Coco's, they headed straight to the famous glass elevator.

"Good morning, Jasper," said Grace. "Could you take us to floor number seven, please? We need to visit the Magical Department Floor. We've got an urgent mission."

Jasper pressed the button and the lift whooshed up and up, coming to a halt with a gentle

TING!

Madame Coco glided forward to greet them.

"Welcome, Magic Dolls," she said. "What can I do for you, today?"

"There's a mermaid in trouble," Holly explained. "We're going to meet her at the Sparkling Shore, but we're worried about how we

enter the Undersea Kingdom."

"Ah! Mermaids," said Madame
Coco, her face lighting up.

She led the Dolls to the
very back of the room. There,
hidden beneath swathes of
curtain, was a little door
they'd never noticed before.
Madame Coco pushed it
open and the Dolls gasped...

"These are magic clothes,"
Madame Coco
explained.

She studied the outfits, then chose a shining blue skirt for Grace, a sea-green one for Holly and a rose-pink one for Lily.

"These are beautiful," said Lily, "but how are they going to help us?"

"When you enter the waters of the Sparkling Shore, you'll find you can breathe underwater and swim like a mermaid," said Madame Coco.

Then she handed each of them a matching top and sparkling hairclips.

"Wow!" gasped Holly, almost lost for words. "These are *amazing!*"

Grace's clothes

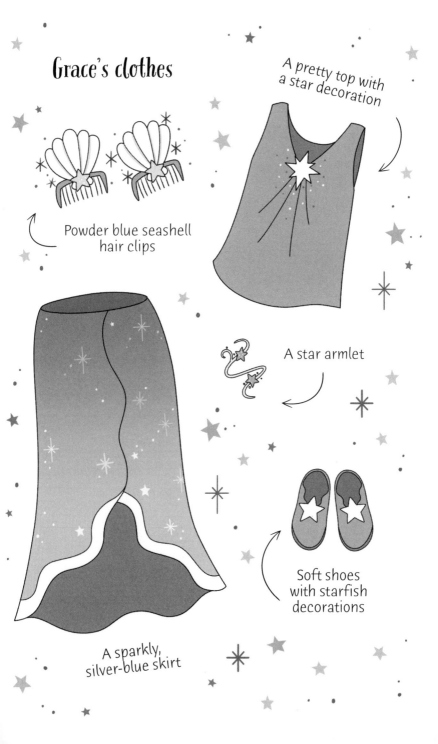

A pretty top with a star decoration

Powder blue seashell hair clips

A star armlet

A sparkly, silver-blue skirt

Soft shoes with starfish decorations

Holly's clothes

A light green top with seaweed details

A turquose seashell hair piece

A wreath woven from seaweed

A flowing sea-green skirt

Cotton shoes with leaf embroidery

Lily's clothes

A floaty, gauzy top with flower decoration

A beautiful rose-pink skirt with a soft wave pattern

A headband with flowers

A pink seashell hair piece

Pretty shoes with flower decorations

The Dolls stepped into the changing rooms. When they stepped out again, they were all beaming.

"Now we're definitely ready for our mission!" said Grace.

"Best of luck," said Madame Coco. "I hope you can help the mermaid…and enjoy the Undersea Kingdom."

The Dolls waved goodbye to Madame Coco and then hurried back across the magical department floor.

They whooshed
down in the lift

TING!

and headed out
onto the sunny
street once more.

"Right!" said
Lily. "Time to go
to the Enchanted
Isle. We just
need to catch
the Shooting
Star train."

She tapped the
symbol on her watch and
a moment later the Shooting
Star drew up beside them in
a cloud of glittering dust.

"Hello, Magic Dolls," said the
train driver, Sienna. "Where can
I take you today?"

"The Sparkling Shore on the Enchanted Isle please, Sienna," said Grace.

Then the Magic Dolls turned to each other. "It's mission go!" said Holly.

Mermaids here we come!

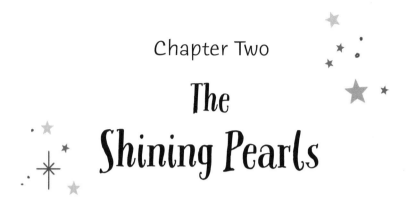

Chapter Two

The
Shining Pearls

The Shooting Star train whizzed through Dolly Town, leaving a trail of glittering sparkles in its wake.

The Dolls saw buildings,
trees and houses flashing
before their eyes.

Then they entered a
dark tunnel, flickering
with hundreds of tiny lights.

With a
WHOOSH
they shot out the other side.

There lay the Enchanted Isle,
its azure blue waters shimmering
in the sunshine.

The train glided to a halt by
the Sparkling Shore, and the Dolls
stepped out onto the sandy beach.

"Thank you, Sienna," said Grace.

"Good luck with your mission, Magic Dolls," Sienna called back, before pulling away in a swirl of sparkling stars.

When the dust had settled, the Dolls turned to see Nerissa, anxiously waiting for them on a rock near the shore, her tail splashing in the foaming waves.

"Thank you so much for coming," said Nerissa. "I didn't know who else to turn to for help."

"We're so glad you called us," said Holly. "What's happened?"

Nerissa looked around, as if to make sure no one was listening.

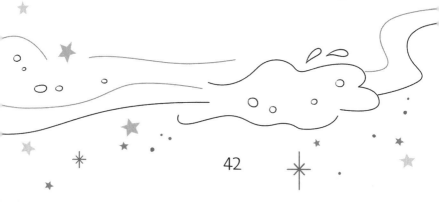

"Tonight is the Grand Undersea Gala," Nerissa started to explain. "It happens once a year. Creatures come from all over the ocean.

There are races...

dancing…

music and feasting.

Everyone in the Undersea

Kingdom is helping prepare for it. I was asked to look after the grand prizes – the three Shining Pearls…" Nerissa stopped speaking suddenly and hung her head.

"What's wrong?" asked Grace, gently.

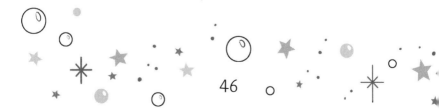

"I've lost the pearls," said
Nerissa, tearfully. "I went to the
Seashell Palace, where the pearls
are kept, but before I could collect
them I was distracted by this
beautiful fish I'd never
seen before.
I swam after
it…and when
I got back the
pearls were
gone!

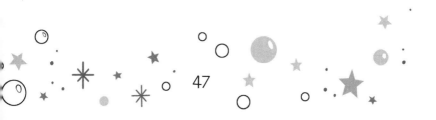

"I haven't told the Mer Queen yet, or any of the other mermaids, as they're so busy getting everything ready and I don't want to worry them. But if there aren't any prizes, the gala will be RUINED. I've tried looking but I can't find them *anywhere*."

Do you think you can help?

"Of course," said Holly.

Lily was already trying to work out what might have happened. "Did anyone else in the palace notice anything strange?" she asked.

"No," said Nerissa, shaking her head. "The palace was deserted. Everyone was busy with the gala. I think someone must have stolen them!"

"In that case," said Lily, "let's start with the room where they went missing. We can search for clues."

"Thank you," said Nerissa.
"I'll take you to the Seashell Palace.
Follow me!" Smiling gratefully at
them, she slipped beneath the waves.

The Dolls followed, each taking
small, tentative steps through
the water.

"Do you think our outfits will really work?" Lily whispered.

But even as she spoke, the waves begin to swirl around the edges of her skirt, and she had a magical tingling feeling.

Holly gasped. She looked at the others and knew they felt it too. One by one, they dived beneath the waves.

"This is amazing," said Holly. "We can breathe underwater… and talk!"

She turned to look over her shoulder. "These outfits really are magical," she said. "Our skirts have become mermaid tails!"

They all turned, admiring their tails, which gleamed like silvery rainbows.

Holly felt at one with the water.
With each flick of her tail, she
glided effortlessly forward.

And the deeper she swam, the more she saw of the mermaids' secret underwater world.

"Look ahead!" said Holly, pointing. "The Seashell Palace. Isn't it beautiful?"

The palace rose from the sea floor, pearly-pink with spiralling seashell turrets.

"In here," said Nerissa, beckoning them in through a side entrance. They swam along deserted corridors until they came to a little room, with a sandy floor, lit by flaming underwater torches.

"This is where the Shining Pearls were," said Nerissa, "in the shell bowl. With the palace empty, *anyone* could have come in and taken them."

"Let's start searching for clues," said Lily. She studied a hole in the wall, high up near the ceiling, while Holly inspected the sandy floor for tracks.

"Someone could have got in through here," said Lily.

"And I think I've found a clue," added Grace, holding up the shell. "There's some slime on the bottom of this shell. Perhaps the thief has left a slimy trail?"

"Have you any idea who that might be?" asked Lily, turning to Nerissa.

Nerissa came over to inspect the slime, her face full of dismay. "I can't believe I didn't spot that!" Her voice was trembling slightly.

Sea Trolls!

"I've never seen a Sea Troll before, but I've heard stories about them. They have slimy skin and leave a trail of slime on whatever they touch. They live in the Deep Sea Caves, beyond the edge of the reef."

"Sea Trolls!" said Holly. "Goodness!"

"I'd be scared to go and visit them on my own," said Nerissa. "The mermaids never visit the Deep Sea Caves and the creatures that live there never

come to the reef. I don't know
why, it's just always been that way."
She looked at the Magic Dolls,
pleadingly. "It could be dangerous
down there. I know it's a lot to
ask, but will you come with me?"

Chapter Three

Diving
Deep

The Magic Dolls didn't hesitate for a moment.

"Of course we will!" said Holly.

"The gala starts when the sun goes down," Nerissa went on. "So we only have a few hours."

"We'll swim as fast as we can," said Lily.

They swam off, following in
Nerissa's wake. She led them
across the reef, over the waving
corals, to where the water grew
darker and colder.

"It's down there," said Nerissa,
pointing to where the sea floor
fell away. The Dolls peered

over the jutting rocks…

and gulped.

"Are you sure about this?"
asked Nerissa.

"We're sure," said Grace,
even though she had a
nervous fluttering in
her tummy.

"Okay," said Nerissa, "here goes."

She swished her tail and dived straight down. The Magic Dolls followed close behind.

They passed strange creatures with long teeth and flashing fins. There were beautiful sharks, too, their bodies weaving from side to side.

At last, they reached the sea
bed, where the rock had worn
away to form underwater
caves on either side.

"It's quite creepy
down here, isn't
it?" whispered
Lily, noticing

the gleaming eyes that stared
out from the black caves.
"Definitely!" agreed Grace.
"The sooner we can find
the pearls and get out
of here, the better."

"Up ahead!" cried Holly, suddenly. "I can see a light. Perhaps it's coming from the Shining Pearls."

Excitedly, they all swam forward. "Oh! I do hope we've found them," said Nerissa. But when they reached the light, they realized it wasn't coming from the pearls at all.

"It's a fish!" said Nerissa, her voice full of disappointment.

"An amazing fish with glowing scales," said Holly, gazing at it.

"But still just a fish," Grace pointed out. "It wouldn't make

much of a prize at the Grand
Undersea Gala."

"No," sighed Nerissa. "We're no closer to finding the pearls and we're running out of time. The Sea Trolls could be anywhere in the Deep Sea!"

"Don't worry," said Grace, as calmly as she could. "If the pearls are here, we'll find them. They'll be sure to shine in the darkness."

By now, Holly had swum a little way ahead and she called out to the others. "There's another cave up here," she said. "And it's glowing!"

They all headed for the cave entrance, Holly a little way in front. Grace trailed her hand along the rocks as she went, then stopped suddenly. "The rock face!" she said. "Feel it! It's slimy. Perhaps we're reaching the home of the Sea Trolls."

Nerissa and Lily stopped to inspect the walls of the rock.

"Holly! Wait!" called Nerissa, but Holly was already at the mouth of the cave.

"Ow!" she cried out suddenly, falling back and clutching her arm.

"What is it?" asked Nerissa, hurrying to her side. "Are you okay?"

Holly pulled a tiny sea thorn from her arm. "I'm fine," she said. "It's just a prickle. It didn't hurt – it was a surprise, that's all."

But then came another, and another. "Oh!" she said, beginning to back away. "I think I'm being attacked. There's definitely something in that cave…and whatever it is, doesn't want to be found!"

Chapter Four

Sea Trolls!

The Magic Dolls and Nerissa waited together a little distance from the cave, just out of firing range of the prickles.

"I'm going to try talking to whoever is attacking us," said Holly. "It has to be worth a try."

"We haven't come to hurt you!" she called out. "We're just looking for some missing pearls." Holly wasn't really expecting an answer, but a voice came back through the darkness.

There are no pearls here, so you can GO AWAY!

"Who said that?" Grace wondered aloud.

They all swam closer again, their curiosity overcoming their fear. And there, at the cave entrance, was a little troll, his hair waving in the current.

"It is a Sea Troll!" Nerissa whispered to the others. "That light must be coming from the pearls. We've found them at last!"

DANGER

Grace looked directly at the Sea Troll, who had now been joined by two more, all of them hovering at the cave entrance.

"Are you *sure* you haven't seen the Shining Pearls?" Grace asked.

"Definitely not," said the second Sea Troll, her hands on her hips. "And you can't come into our cave to check."

"What's more," added the third troll, "if you don't leave, we're going to fire more prickles at you. So there!"

"What shall we do?" Lily whispered to the others. "The Sea Trolls are only small. Shall we just swim into the cave and look? There's definitely something glowing in there."

But Nerissa was shaking her head. "Sea Trolls aren't small," she whispered back.

"Yes they are," said Grace, puzzled. "They're much smaller than us!"

"That's because they're *young ones*," said Nerissa. "A grown Sea Troll is much…"

"…BIGGER!" boomed a voice behind them.

"Hooray!" chanted the little Sea Trolls. "Mummy and Daddy are back!"

Nerissa and the Magic Dolls turned to see two ENORMOUS Sea Trolls behind them. And they didn't look happy.

Summoning all her courage, Holly began to speak. "Excuse me," she said. "We're hoping you might be able to help. The Shining Pearls have gone missing from the Seashell Palace. They're meant to be the prizes at the Grand Undersea Gala, but we can't find them anywhere. We noticed there's something glowing in your cave and we wondered if we might be able to take a look…"

Holly's voice tailed off under the stern stare of the Sea Trolls.

Why should we care about the Undersea Gala? It's not as if we're ever allowed to go.

"And it's always so dark down here, we hardly get any light. Even if we did have your Shining Pearls, we wouldn't give them back."

"It doesn't have to be that way…" began Nerissa. But the trolls weren't interested. They brushed past Nerissa and the Magic Dolls and began making their way towards the cave.

"Wait!" said Holly.

KEEP X OUT!!

The Sea Trolls turned.
Holly whispered something
to Nerissa, who nodded in
agreement. "Why don't
you come to the gala
tonight?" said Holly. "The
mermaids would love to
have you."

"Ha!" scoffed Father Sea
Troll. "Why should we
believe you? We know
you're only interested
in the pearls."

"We *do* want the pearls back," said Nerissa, "but you really are welcome at the gala. It's the one time of year everyone in the ocean comes together. Please, join us."

But the Sea Trolls were unmoved.

"Leave," growled Father Sea Troll. "Before we make you."

Chapter Five

Surprise Guests at the Gala

Nerissa and the Magic Dolls swam back to the reef in silence.

"It was so kind of you to help," smiled Nerissa, although the Dolls could tell how anxious she was about the pearls. "I'll tell the Mer Queen about the Sea Trolls. It's sad they don't feel welcome among the mermaids.

And I'll have to tell her that I've lost the Shining Pearls, too. I just hope it doesn't ruin the gala."

"But we can't just give up," said Lily. "Maybe we should find something else to give as a prize?"

"We could look for seashells?" said Grace. "Or flowers?"

"That's a wonderful idea," said Nerissa. "It won't make up for the missing pearls, but it's better than nothing. There are magical flowers on the edge of the reef that re-grow as soon as they're picked. Let's gather some on our way to the gala."

As soon as they reached the reef, the Magic Dolls began to pick armfuls of the magical flowers.

"That should be enough," said Nerissa. "We must hurry. The gala will be starting soon."

They swam as fast as they could towards the Seashell Palace.

"It looks so beautiful!" cried Lily.

The palace was lit with hundreds of underwater lanterns, which gave the sea a magical glow. And swimming towards the palace, like a river of life, were creatures from all over the ocean.

A group of mermaids, playing lilting music on seashell harps, were joined by a band of trumpeting seahorses.

"That's the signal," whispered Nerissa. "The Mer Queen is about to arrive."

As she spoke, there was a ripple in the current and the Mer Queen rode out of her palace on a silver dolphin, her long hair flowing behind her.

"Welcome, everyone, to the Undersea Gala!" the Mer Queen announced to the crowds.

As the sea creatures began to cheer, Nerissa whispered to the Magic Dolls. "I can't leave it any longer," she said. "I'll swim over to the Mer Queen now and tell her about the missing pearls."

"Wait!" said Lily, holding her back. "Over there! At the edge of the reef…"

They all turned to look, and there, rising up from the deep, were the family of Sea Trolls.

They strode over the white
sands towards Nerissa and
the Magic Dolls.

"Have they come to cause trouble?" Lily wondered aloud. "They seemed so certain they didn't want to come to the gala…"

But when the Sea Trolls reached them, they didn't look quite so scary any more. "We've changed our minds," said Mother Sea Troll, gruffly. "We'd like to watch the gala, if we're still invited."

She looked directly at Nerissa. "You said we really would be welcome. Is that true?"

"Of course!" said Nerissa.

"Everyone will be so glad you came," added Holly, beaming.

"We'd like to give you these," said Father Sea Troll. He put out his enormous fist and slowly uncurled his fingers. There, in the palm of his hand, were the Shining Pearls. The Magic Dolls gasped as they saw them properly for the first time. They really were

beautiful – lit by their own glow,
casting a ray of golden light.

"We're sorry we stole them
from you. We wanted something
beautiful to light up our dark cave.
Our children found them when
they were exploring your palace,
but it was wrong for us to have
kept them."

"We're sorry, too," said one of

the little Sea Trolls, peeping out from behind her father. "We promise we won't fire prickles at you again."

"Thank you for bringing back the pearls," said Nerissa.

At that moment, they were joined by the Mer Queen.

"How wonderful that you're here," she said. "We've never had Sea Trolls at the Undersea Gala before. We thought you preferred the Deep Sea."

"Not *always*," said Nerissa, smiling at them.

"Well," said the Mer Queen. "Today you will be our honoured guests."

"Hooray!" said the little Sea Trolls.

"Thank you," said Father Sea Troll, in his deep rumble.

"Will you show them to their seats, Nerissa?" asked the Mer Queen.

"Of course," Nerissa replied. "And before you go – can I introduce you to the Magic Dolls? This is Holly, and Grace, and Lily. They've been helping me prepare for the gala."

"Thank you, Magic Dolls," said the Mer Queen, smiling at them. "I do hope you'll stay too?"

We'd *love* to!

"I'd better go now and see to our other guests," said the Mer Queen. "But I leave you in safe hands."

As the Mer Queen swam gracefully away, Nerissa showed the Sea Trolls to their seats.

"We'd also like to give you these, in welcome," said Nerissa. And she handed the Sea Trolls the flowers they'd gathered from the reef.

"Thank you," said Mother Sea Troll. "We'll treasure these."

Silence fell over the crowds once

more, as the Mer Queen made her
next announcement.

"Everyone, take your places!
It's time for the races!"

"Oh!" gasped Grace. "Look! I
can't believe it! Unicorns of the Sea!"

There were five of them,
glowing silvery grey in the light
of the flaming torches. Each had a
rider on its back, and when the
Mer Queen blew on her seashell
horn, they set off, speeding along
the race track.

They were followed by

a seahorse race…

...and then an amazing display. Fish and mermaids danced though the water to music.

Next came an octopus, performing magic tricks.

And last of all, an undersea feast.

"Before you eat," said the Mer Queen, "I would like to present the prizes."

The crowds gasped as Nerissa passed the Shining Pearls to the Queen. She presented the first pearl to the winning merboy and his Sea Unicorn, the next to

the winner of the Seahorse Race.
The last pearl went to the best
dancing mermaid.

The crowds burst into cheers.

The Magic Dolls turned and
grinned at each other. "I'm so glad
we got the pearls back," said Lily.

"Me too," said Grace. "But
sadly, I think it's time for us to go."

"Oh! Must you really leave?" asked Nerissa.

"I'm afraid we must," said Holly. "We never know when we'll be called on our next mission. But thank you for letting us stay for the gala."

They waved to the Sea Trolls, who were enjoying a delicious seaweed salad and then went to say goodbye to the Mer Queen.

"Nerissa told me how you helped today," said the Mer Queen. "We're so grateful to you all – not just for retrieving the Shining Pearls, but for bringing us together with the Sea Trolls."

"It was our pleasure," said Holly.

"I would like to give each of you a gift, to say thank you," said the Mer Queen, and she handed them each

 a beautiful necklace, made up of a row of tiny, glowing shells.

"If you're ever near water, and you need our help, just blow on these seashells and we will come to you."

"Thank you so much," said Lily.

"And remember to call us, if you ever need help again," said Grace. "We've loved our time in your Undersea Kingdom."

They gave Nerissa one last hug goodbye, then headed for the surface.

Chapter Six

Cupcake Café

The Magic Dolls swam until they reached the shore, where their tails became beautiful skirts once more, swirling around their legs. They stepped out of the water, magically dry in the warm night air.

Holly gazed back down at the

gently lapping waves. "Isn't it amazing," she said, "to think there's a whole underwater world down there. I hope we can visit again soon."

Grace tapped the star symbol on her watch and moments later,

the Shooting Star appeared in a
haze of glimmering dust.

"Greetings, Magic Dolls," said
Sienna. "How was your mission?"

"Successful!" said Lily, grinning.

"Amazing!" said Holly.

"We'd like to go to the Cupcake Café to celebrate please!" said Grace, as they stepped aboard.

"Cupcake Café coming up!" called Sienna. The doors glided shut and the Shooting Star began to whoosh away.

The Dolls gazed out of the window as they sped along the coast.

"Look!" said Grace. "The dragons are waking from their long sleep! I can see them, flying through the sky."

They had one tantalizing glimpse of a flock of dragons, flapping their brightly-coloured wings, before the Shooting Star whooshed into the tunnel, and the Enchanted Isle disappeared from view.

"I wonder what our next mission will be?" said Grace, as they drew up beside the Cupcake Café.

"I don't mind, as long as we have time for a hot chocolate first!" laughed Lily.

They took their seats in their favourite cosy corner at the back.

"What a mission!" said Holly. "We helped a mermaid…"

"…saw Unicorns of the Sea," added Grace.

"And made friends with Sea Trolls," said Lily.

They each put out a hand, laying them one on top of the other. "Magic Dolls forever!" they chanted. "Until next time…"

The End

Join the **Magic Dolls**
on their next adventure in

Read on for a sneak peek…

I t was a bright, sunny day in Dolly Town and the Magic Dolls were sitting in their garden.

"I can't stop thinking about our last mission to the Enchanted Isle," said Holly. "It was so amazing to meet the mermaids…"

"I wonder what our next mission will be…" said Lily. "Will it be to help the unicorns again? Or the fairies?"

"We're about to find out," said Holly. "Look!"

All their watches had started flashing.

There's a
baby dragon
in TROUBLE
on the Enchanted Isle.
He's only recently hatched
and his parents are nowhere to
be seen... Do you think you could
look after the baby dragon until
his parents return?

Edited by Lesley Sims and Stephanie King
Designed by Hannah Cobley

First published in 2020 by Usborne Publishing Ltd.,
Usborne House, 83-85 Saffron Hill, London EC1N 8RT, England.
usborne.com Copyright © 2020 Usborne Publishing Ltd. UKE